CAST

CAST A DARK SHADOW

Julie Coffin

CHIVERS
THORNDIKE

This Large Print book is published by BBC Audiobooks Ltd, Bath, England and by Thorndike Press®, Waterville, Maine, USA.

Published in 2006 in the U.K. by arrangement with the author.

Published in 2006 in the U.S. by arrangement with Julie Coffin.

U.K. Hardcover   ISBN 1–4056–3667–X (Chivers Large Print)
U.K. Softcover   ISBN 1–4056–3689–0 (Camden Large Print)
U.S. Softcover   ISBN 0–7862–8186–3 (British Favorites)

The text of this Large Print edition is unabridged.
Other aspects of the book may vary from the original edition.

Set in 16 pt. New Times Roman.

Printed in Great Britain on acid-free paper.

British Library Cataloguing in Publication Data available

Library of Congress Cataloging-in-Publication Data

Coffin, Julie.
    Cast a dark shadow / by Julie Coffin.—Large print ed.
       p.   cm.
    ISBN 0–7862–8186–3 (lg. print : sc : alk. paper)
    1. Large type books. I. Title.
    PR6053.O3C37 2005
    823'.914—dc22   2005023949

CHAPTER ONE

Blazing higher and higher, the bonfire sent a trail of sparks shooting up into the dark sky, as Abigail tossed on yet another page of a past memory.

Tomorrow I shall probably regret what I've done, she thought.

Just one last bundle of letters remained. For a moment, she was tempted to read them once more. Then, closing her eyes she threw them deep into the flames. The edges blackened, curling slowly, before they sank down into the embers and crumbled away.

The tears that stung her cheeks, she told herself fiercely, were caused by the billowing, acrid smoke, nothing more. She'd cried too many tears in the past months for there to be any left. Marc was gone, their marriage finally ended. Miranda had won.

Miranda!

With the toe of her boot, Abigail edged a smouldering fragment back into the fire. Miranda—a mermaid's name. Well, she'd certainly lured Marc.

The fact that he had a wife and child didn't mean anything to her, or to Marc, Abigail thought. How could he do such a thing? I hate him, hate him, hate him. Only I don't! I wish I did. Maybe then it wouldn't hurt so much.

1

She watched the flames flicker and die down. Soon, just a pile of grey ash would be left, all that remained of their love.

Should I have kept just one letter, she wondered, to remember how much Marc once loved me?

With the heat of the flames gone, Abigail shivered. Frost sparkled on the lawn and the grass was crisp under her feet as she turned to walk towards the house.

Opening the kitchen door, she looked back into the garden. A tiny crimson glow shimmered for a second, and vanished. Abigail tugged off her boots. The house was silent. Flora was asleep in her bedroom upstairs.

She tiptoed up the stairs, pausing at her daughter's open door to peep in. The child slept, one hand curled round the ear of a blue rabbit. Back in her own bedroom, Abigail lifted a suitcase down from the top of her wardrobe and began to pack waiting piles of clothes into it.

Next day was a new day, a new life, she thought as she eventually fell into bed and a deep sleep.

Abigail sat up in bed, trying to convince herself of that. It was still dark. She glanced at the little clock on the bedside cabinet, its figures glowing. Almost seven o'clock. In an hour's time, they'd leave. By then she would have loaded up the car and given Flora her breakfast.

It was strange to be spending Christmas away from home. All five years of her married life had been spent there. Abigail had tried to refuse to change her plans, but Great-Aunt Holly was determined.

'I insist, Abigail,' Great-Aunt Holly's voice had boomed from the telephone earlier in the month. 'I shall be eighty-five on Christmas Day. I expect all my family to be there, every member. I have an extremely important announcement to make.'

'But the weather could be awful by then, Great-Aunt,' Abigail protested. 'Besides, it's nearly three hundred miles to drive, and there's Flora.'

'Nonsense! When I was twice your age, I thought nothing of driving from here in Cornwall right up to Scotland,' her great-aunt retorted. 'Start out early and leave yourself plenty of time. The child will love the trip. I'll expect you here for tea on the twenty-third. Goodbye.'

The conversation was over. Great-Aunt Holly had given her orders!

Abigail had to admit she was curious. What announcement could it be? Every member of the family to be present, Great-Aunt Holly said. Abigail tried to think who they were. Her great-aunt had been widowed very early in her married life and had no children, so they must be those of her brothers and sisters, and their children.

It was years since Abigail had visited. She'd been about six or seven, only a couple of years older than Flora was now. She tried to remember that time.

Her parents had taken her there. They'd been on holiday in the West Country, touring. The house was huge, like a castle, with dozens and dozens of rooms, or so it seemed then to Abigail. Lots of stairs, too, and the sea, so close, the sound of it booming through the granite walls, echoing.

Since then, Great-Aunt Holly had sent cards over the years, for birthdays, Christmas, each with a book token enclosed. Abigail used to stick the card inside each volume she bought.

Great-Aunt Holly hadn't come to her wedding. Too old and too far, she'd written on the note enclosed in a box of six silver teaspoons.

Carrying the suitcase out to the car, Abigail heaved it into the boot. Flora was still asleep. Abigail took their wellingtons from under the stairs, unhooked their anoraks from pegs in the hall and added them as well.

Anything else, she wondered, scraping ice from the windscreen.

'Don't leave me behind, Mummy!'

Flora, almost tripping over the hem of her nightie, ran through the open front door, her eyes wide with alarm, the blue rabbit clutched to her chest.

'Darling! Of course I won't leave you.'

4

Abigail caught the little girl up in her arms and hugged her.

'I'm just loading the car, that's all.'

The child buried her face into Abigail's neck and her voice was muffled.

'I thought you were going away without me.'

Abigail's arms tightened.

'I'd never ever do that, darling,' she said, kissing the top of her daughter's head.

'Daddy did.'

'I never will.'

She lowered Flora to the ground and took hold of her hand.

'Come on. As soon as we've eaten our breakfast, we'll be off.'

CHAPTER TWO

'Are we nearly there yet?' Flora wailed from the back of the car. 'Blue Bun's very tired.'

'Poor old Blue Bun,' Abigail replied. 'Why don't you both have a little sleep? By the time you wake up, we'll probably be there.'

They'd stopped twice on the journey, in Dorchester for coffee, orange juice and buns, and again farther on for lunch.

Although only just gone three o'clock, the sun had set in a dazzle of brilliance, painting the sky with a myriad shades of pink, lilac and red, before disappearing. Abigail didn't fancy driving along unfamiliar roads in the dark. She was tired, too.

Steering the car into a layby, she switched on the interior light and studied the map. They'd crossed Bodmin Moor a few miles back. Any moment now should be a right turn. Abigail slipped the car into gear and eased out on to the road again.

Half an hour later, she knew she was lost. In the headlights, every narrow lane looked the same, high-banked and winding, but she was sure they'd passed a certain tumbledown barn before.

Thankfully, Flora was asleep, but for how long? She was sure to wake and need a toilet soon.

In the distance Abigail could see the long beam of a lighthouse stream out at regular intervals.

I can't be far from the sea, she decided, and Great-Aunt Holly's house. There had been signposts pointing the way until she reached a crossroads, then nothing.

She'd tried three directions, without success, and this one was her last hope.

The lane dipped suddenly into a hollow and she noticed an even narrower track twisting sharply away from it. Through skeleton trees, Abigail saw the square outline of lighted windows. Gateposts loomed, white against the night.

She turned the car through them. A drive,

full of unexpected potholes, wound its way under overhanging branches that scraped every now and then against the roof.

Abigail drove slowly, bumping over the rough ground. And then the house was there, right in front of her. Twin security lights snapped on, dazzling her eyes. Flora stirred and lifted her head.

'I can't find Blue Bun.'

The front door opened, sending a carpet of brightness flooding out, and two silhouettes stood waiting. Abigail climbed stiffly from the car and opened the rear door to undo Flora's seat-belt. Blue Bun fell on to the gravel and was swiftly retrieved.

'Darlings!'

A tall, straight-backed figure came down the front steps, arms outstretched.

'Hello, Great-Aunt Holly,' Abigail said. 'This is Flora.'

'Don't leave them out there in the cold, Holly, my love. They'll catch their deaths.'

Carrying Flora up the steps, Abigail glanced in surprise when she heard the firm male voice.

A white-haired man, as straight-backed as her great-aunt, hustled them into the hallway, and closed the door.

'So you're Abigail, and this must be little Flora? Well, Holly, introduce me.'

'All in good time, William! Let them get inside the house first. Now, my dears, we're just about to start tea. I'm sure you must be dying for a cup of refreshment.'

Feeling slightly dazed, Abigail lowered Flora to the ground and together they followed her great-aunt into a room filled with people.

As they entered, there was a sudden silence and every face turned in their direction. Abigail let her gaze travel round. At first, all seemed to be strangers, until . . .

Abigail's heart jerked as if missing a beat.

Sitting in a red velvet chair, close to the fireplace, was a woman Abigail recognised only too well, and beside her . . .

With a shriek of delight, Flora let go of her mother's hand and ran across the room.

'Daddy! Daddy! Mummy didn't tell me you'd be here, too.'

CHAPTER THREE

The shock of seeing Marc again after all this time was like a bucket of water being tipped over her.

Abigail thought briefly that she was dreaming, until she heard him gasp and realised that Flora's arms were clinging so tightly to his neck, he must be choking.

Then she became aware of Miranda's eyes, like emerald splinters, narrowed, staring at her. There was shock, too, on her face.

But what are they doing here, Abigail asked herself. Was it some horrible trick of Great-Aunt Holly's, bringing us all together, like this?

'You know each other?'

Her great-aunt's voice, she noticed, was full of surprise.

'Marc is my ex-husband, and Miranda is his girlfriend.

'Oh, my poor child! I had no idea!'

Abigail was about to ask a question, but her great-aunt answered it for her.

'Miranda is William's daughter.'

Abigail was beginning to get confused.

'Who is William?' she asked.

'I'm so sorry, my dear, I haven't properly introduced him yet, have I? William lives here, with me. I suppose, in modern day terms, you would call us an item.'

Momentarily, Abigail thought her great-aunt must be joking. After all, they were both in their eighties!

'You can fall in love at any age, you know, my dear. It's not reserved merely for the young.'

'No,' Abigail stammered. 'I suppose not.'

'You sound disbelieving. Never mind, I'll tell you all about it later. Now, tea should be ready. Ring that bell, will you, dear? Would Flora prefer milk or a soft drink?'

9

Later, Abigail carefully put their folded clothes into drawers and tucked the empty case under her bed. She'd never slept in one like this before, a four-poster, draped in faded material that looked as though, if touched, it would crumble into fine dust.

Flora was already asleep in a small bed on the other side of the room, Blue Bun tucked in beside her. Abigail had decided it was better than having the child on her own in a room across the corridor.

Earlier, Flora had insisted on sitting on her daddy's lap to eat tea. Knowing how difficult her little daughter could be on occasions, Abigail was worried there would be a scene when it came to bedtime, but Marc had carried her upstairs and read her a story.

Like he used to, Abigail thought, before Miranda came on the scene. She wondered what Miranda must be feeling. Is she as stunned as I am, to find us all here together?

While everyone ate tea, trying to balance cups, saucers and plates on their laps, Abigail had glanced round, not knowing who any of them were. Some, she'd decided, must be William's relations. Great-Aunt Holly had reeled off names, but Abigail was feeling too shattered to take them in. All she wanted was to escape to her own bedroom and try to work out how she was going to cope for the next few days.

She'd stayed upstairs with Flora for the evening. The first night in a strange house, especially such a large and old one, was bound to be bewildering for a small child. A couple of minutes before eight o'clock, the housekeeper had bought up a large tray with carrot and parsnip soup, thick slices of gammon and salad, and a glass bowl of fresh peaches.

'I hope this'll be all right for you, Mrs Dale. There's coffee in the insulated jug. I wasn't sure if the little girl would still be awake, so I've put a pot of yoghurt and a couple of biscuits just in case. If there's anything else you need, ring down on that phone over there.'

An hour later, she returned to collect the empty dishes, by which time Abigail had showered and was exhausted, ready for bed.

Surprisingly, she went straight to sleep, waking only when Flora climbed in beside her, snuggled under the covers and began to chatter.

'Is it tonight Father Christmas comes, Mummy? Will he know I'm in this house and not in ours?'

Her questions rushed on, one after another, not giving Abigail a chance to answer. She had so many questions of her own that needed a reply. Suddenly, Flora slid her feet from the covers and ran across to the door.

'I'll go and see Daddy now.'

'No! Wait, darling. We don't know which

room he's in,' Abigail said quickly, catching hold of the back of her nightie, not wanting the little girl to find him and Miranda together.

'Let's get dressed and then you can see him at breakfast.'

Pouting, the child came slowly back across the room.

'I shall wear my bestest dress, the sparkly one. Daddy hasn't seen that,' she muttered.

'Maybe your jeans and blue sweatshirt would be better, darling. You'll want to explore the beach, won't you? After breakfast,' she added.

'With Daddy,' Flora said firmly.

Breakfast was a formal, old-fashioned meal. The long dining-room table was covered with a starched white cloth. Places were set with heavy, ornate cutlery and mats picturing hunting scenes.

On the sideboard were silver-domed covers over dishes of bacon, sausages, kidneys, mushrooms, tomatoes and eggs cooked in various ways. Tall jugs of fruit juices and packets of cereals stood beside small glasses and bowls.

Abigail and Flora were the first down. They'd just filled their bowls with cornflakes when the door opened again and a tall, rather thin man with tousled, windswept hair came in to join them.

'Hi,' he said, pouring grapefruit juice into a

glass then, raising each cover in turn, he loaded a plate with food from the silver dishes.

'I'm Luke, by the way, one of William's grandchildren.'

Is he Miranda's brother, Abigail wondered.

'Have you brought a stocking to hang up?' Flora enquired, wiping her mouth with a stiff, linen napkin.

'Actually it's a long grey sock,' Luke said gravely. 'Do you think Father Christmas will mind?'

Flora wrinkled her nose.

'Well, it is supposed to be a stocking, but I 'spect he'll fill it just the same.'

She began to butter a slice of toast.

'At our house, we have a Christmas tree and Father Christmas puts the big presents under that, but there isn't one here. What do you think he'll do about that?'

Her eyes were worried as she gazed at Luke.

'He won't take the presents away again, will he?'

Luke leaned forward across the table towards her and dropped his voice to a whisper.

'Are you good at keeping secrets, Flora?'

The little girl nodded vigorously.

'Well, I've just been out for a walk and coming back, I saw a simply ginormous Christmas tree out on the terrace. I think someone will bring it indoors later today and everyone can decorate it.'

13

Flora's mouth curved into a wide smile.

'Really, really ginormous?'

Luke nodded.

'Really, really ginormous. It might even be too big to come through the front door. After you've eaten your breakfast, how would you like to come and see it?'

He paused and turned to look at Abigail.

'That is, if your mummy says you can.'

'Well,' Flora said slowly, studying his face, 'I'm not allowed to go anywhere with a stranger, even if they look very, very nice and kind, like you do.'

'Then perhaps your mummy could come with us. Will you, Abigail?' Luke asked so kindly.

Abigail nodded, surprised he remembered her name and, as if reading her thoughts, he smiled.

'Don't forget, there was only one of you when we were all introduced yesterday.'

Other members of the family were beginning to stroll into the room, filling plates and chattering together.

Everyone seems to know each other, Abigail noticed, feeling on the edge of the group, until Luke continued talking to her, asking where she lived and what sort of journey they'd had.

Last to arrive were Miranda and Marc. Whereas all the others were dressed in old jumpers or sweatshirts, jeans or trousers, Miranda's red suede jacket, white polo-necked jumper and black trousers made her look as though she'd stepped straight from the pages of some glamorous fashion magazine.

Like she always does, Abigail thought enviously.

She'd only seen Miranda on a few occasions, but each time the other woman looked immaculate.

Was that what attracted Marc, Abigail asked herself, glancing down at her own, rather matted navy jumper and faded jeans. *After all, she's a complete contrast to me, without a doubt.*

'Daddy!'

Flora left her chair and scampered round the table to join her father. Abigail watched as he kissed the little girl, feeling a shaft of pain spear through her. Once, he would have been kissing both of them at the breakfast table.

'Come back and finish your scrambled eggs, Flora.'

The words snapped out and Abigail saw her daughter's eyes widen with surprise, before her small forehead folded into a frown.

'I'm going to eat it here with my daddy.'

Those surrounding her at the table stopped eating and Abigail was conscious that they were looking to see what would happen next. Knowing that Flora might erupt into a tantrum if she ordered the child back to her seat, Abigail wasn't quite sure how to react. Then Luke leaned slowly forward.

15

'Don't forget the you-know-what.'

He winked one eye at Flora.

'It might disappear if we don't go out there soon.'

Flora hesitated, thought quietly for a second, then slid from her father's lap, ran back to her place and rapidly began to spoon up the scrambled egg.

'Thank you,' Abigail whispered in Luke's ear. 'From that devious bit of distraction, you obviously have children of your own.'

He grinned back at her, fine lines crinkling the corners of his eyes.

'Quite a few, to be honest!'

'But you haven't brought them with you?'

Luke picked up the coffee jug.

'No. I think they would be a little too much for Holly.'

'Are they very young then?' Abigail asked.

'Some of them are,' he said rather mysteriously. 'More coffee?' he added, changing the subject.

He refilled her cup and turned to do the same for the lady next to him. Abigail was intrigued. Luke didn't look all that old, early thirties maybe, and yet he made it sound as though he had a large family.

Perhaps he's remarried and his new partner has children of her own to add to his, Abigail thought. Strange that she's not here with him for Christmas, though. He seems too caring to abandon anyone. But then, people aren't always as they appear on the surface.

Flora caught the sleeve of his sweatshirt and tugged it.

'I've eaten every bit now,' she said. 'Can we go outside and find the you-know-what?'

Her words ended in a gurgle of laughter.

'Put some warm clothes on first,' Luke replied. 'It's very frosty out there and we wouldn't want you catching cold, now, would we?'

'Come on then, Mummy.'

As they passed Marc's chair, he put out a hand to detain Abigail.

'Yes?' she said, stopping.

'Miranda and I need to have an urgent word with you some time. Perhaps later, when you come back? It's something we want to get settled once and for all.'

Her back stiffened at the odd tone of his voice. It was hesitant, almost wary, but Marc was always so positive, never wary. His eyes refused to look into hers.

Abigail transferred her gaze to Miranda, sitting next to him, aware that the woman was watching her very closely.

Is it from jealousy, or something else, she wondered, then saw a tiny smile flicker the corners of Miranda's perfect mouth. Nervousness, Abigail asked herself, or triumph?

'Can't we talk now?' she asked.

'Later,' Marc repeated abruptly, and turned

17

his back on her.

CHAPTER FOUR

'There are heaps of thick jackets in the lobby. Borrow one of those,' Great-Aunt Holly suggested, when she met Abigail and Flora coming down the stairs. 'It's freezing outside. Those cagoules will never be warm enough. You'll find some scarves, too. Wrap one of them round Flora.'

With a borrowed sheepskin jacket on top of her own anorak and having wound a long scarf over Flora's hood, round her neck and across her chest, then tied at the back, Abigail opened the lobby door into the garden.

An icy blast of wind almost swung it off its hinges and for a second Abigail fought to close it again. Luke was already on the terrace, stamping his feet and slapping his hands together. Flora broke away from her mother and ran towards him.

'Is it still there?'

Luke bent down and lifted her up.

'Look!'

He pointed to where an immense fir tree was leaning against the side wall, its branches swaying in the wind.

'It's 'normous!' Flora breathed. 'Will it really fit indoors?'

'We'll have to see, won't we?' Luke replied. 'Do you want to have a quick trot down to the sea, or is it too cold?'

Flora looked at her mother.

'Can we, Mummy? Please?'

With the fury of the wind biting into her, Abigail wanted to refuse and hurry back into the warmth of the house, but the pleading in Flora's eyes was too much.

'Not for long,' she replied, and followed them to where a gravel path twisted away through woodland.

The ground was hard with frost, every blade of grass edged in white. Abigail hunched her chin into the sheepskin collar of her jacket and wished she'd borrowed one of the thick scarves as well. Luke was striding ahead, with Flora giggling and bouncing on his shoulders, her mittened hands clenched round his forehead.

The path suddenly ended at a sturdy, stone wall, and then their feet were crunching over a shingle beach. High, granite rocks rose on either side, forming a sheltered cove. With eyes blurred and stinging from the wind, Abigail stood facing a grey sea that stretched endlessly to merge with an even greyer sky. It was impossible to decide where one ended and the other began.

Heavy waves, white-capped and mountainous, thundered in across a stretch of dark, wet sand. Shining strands of seaweed coiled along its edge, seized every now and then to be dragged back into the foam. Abigail shivered.

'You're frozen, and so am I,' Luke said, and Abigail saw that the tips of his ears glowed scarlet through his tousled hair.

Flora looked to be the only warm one, her rosy face almost hidden in the soft, woollen folds of the scarf. With the wind on their backs, they began to climb up through the garden.

Bare branches of trees whipped to and fro, some giving ominous creaks. Abigail worried all the time that a piece might crash down and was glad when they reached the safety of the terrace again.

'Oh, it's gone!'

Flora's voice was full of disappointment and Abigail saw that the fir tree no longer leaned against the wall.

'I expect it's been taken indoors,' Luke comforted Flora, pushing open the lobby door and sitting the little girl down on a bench to tug off her wellingtons.

Abigail unknotted and unwound the scarf, then unbuttoned her own heavy jacket and put it on a peg, to join years of old coats hanging there. Running on ahead, while she and Luke walked more slowly back along the corridor, Flora let out a shriek of excitement.

'It's in here! Come and see.'

At one end of the lounge, on the opposite side of the room from the huge, open fireplace, stood the Christmas tree. Its roots were now in half a barrel filled with earth and its top branch almost touched the high, beamed ceiling. Abigail breathed the sharp, intense smell of pine. She'd never seen such an enormous tree.

To Flora it must seem like a giant. Just then, Great-Aunt Holly came in, carrying a large, cardboard box. Festoons of sparkling tinsel hung round her neck, reaching almost to her knees.

'Now,' she said, 'who is going to help me decorate this?'

'Me, me, me!' Flora shouted at once, jumping up and down, unable to contain her excitement.

'Right then, Luke, you go and fetch the step-ladder. One of the gardeners should have left it in the lobby by now.'

Great-Aunt Holly put the box on the floor and added the tinsel.

'Flora, find the rest of the children. They ought to have finished their breakfasts, and if they haven't, it's high time they did. We'll need a couple of the older boys to go up the ladder.'

She turned to Abigail.

'Marc's looking for you, dear. Needs to chat about something, he said. I told him to wait in the morning-room. It's on the far side of the hall, beyond the front door.'

Seeing that Flora was quite happy helping with the tree, Abigail left her and went to find the morning-room. What on earth can Marc want to discuss, she wondered. Everything had been settled, the decree absolute granted. Their marriage was over.

*   *   *

A wood fire was blazing in the wide, brick grate. As Abigail opened the door and walked into the room, one log settled and a shower of sparks rose up the chimney. Seeing them reminded her of the bonfire, when she'd burned all Marc's love letters, only the day before.

He was standing by the window, his back towards her. The sight brought back so many memories, the way his hair peaked down to the collar of his shirt, the shape of his ears, the firm line of his neck. She closed her eyes, remembering the feel of his skin under her caressing fingers, how his mouth would close over hers. Her breathing quickened.

'Won't you sit down, Abigail?'

The soft voice came from behind her. Abigail swung round to see Miranda sitting, elegant legs crossed, in a deep armchair. Marc turned away from the window, but his eyes didn't meet hers.

'You have something to discuss?' she said. 'I thought everything was sorted out, finished.'

He cleared his throat. A nervous habit, she recalled, when he wasn't sure quite what to

22

say. Her body tensed.

'Miranda and I . . .' he began, and cleared his throat again.

'Oh, do get on!' Miranda said impatiently.

Marc glared across the room at her.

'Miranda and I are to be married early in the new year.'

Stung by the words, Abigail snapped back.

'Well, you certainly don't waste any time, do you? The ink is hardly dry on the final decree. How many days ago was it granted? Two, or have I miscounted?'

'There's no need to be bitter, Abigail.'

'Bitter? Oh, I'm not bitter. Amazed, maybe, but not bitter.'

She forced her eyes to rake up and down Miranda's slim figure, determined to stay outwardly calm.

'Why the hurry? I take it a birth is not imminent.'

'Don't be so coarse! That's not like you, Abigail.'

'Maybe I've had reason to change, Marc.'

She breathed deeply, trying to stay calm.

'Was that all you had to tell me?'

Marc chewed his lower lip and cleared his throat again.

'No,' he said slowly, and then continued in a rush of words. 'When Miranda and I are married, we're applying for custody of Flora.'

In the silence of the room, Abigail was conscious of the sound of her own heartbeat.

23

'Custody of Flora?' she managed to say, each word coming separately, wrapped in horror.

'We can provide a permanent home for her, Abigail, give her complete security.'

'She has a permanent home, and complete security,' Abigail snapped back.

Miranda's voice cut in softly.

'A two-bedroom, little terrace house, Abigail, with a handkerchief-size scrap of garden? And you work, don't you? Who looks after Flora when you're not around?'

Abigail turned her stunned, tear-filled gaze on the beautiful woman curled into the armchair.

'That little terraced house, as you call it, is our home, and I had no other choice but to work when Marc left.'

A tear spilled over and slid slowly down Abigail's cheek. Angrily, she brushed it away as she continued.

'Flora's with a child-minder during the day. She's one of my friends. She loves her. Flora's happy.'

Adjusting a cushion into a more comfortable position behind her back, Miranda went on.

'But we can provide so much, Abigail. For instance, a beautiful, spacious home, acres of garden, maybe a pony as she grows older, a good private school, a mother and a father.'

'You'll never be Flora's mother.'

'Children adapt very rapidly, Abigail, and they forget,' Miranda said rather flippantly.

In desperation, Abigail turned back to Marc.

'You can't really mean to do this, Marc. You couldn't be so cruel.'

His eyes still refused to look into hers.

'She's my daughter, too, Abigail.'

Catching hold of his arms, she shook him.

'But you haven't even seen her for months! She couldn't understand why you'd left her, Marc. It almost destroyed her. Only recently has she begun to settle down again.'

'Well, she won't be upset any longer, will she, Abigail? Once Miranda and I have custody, she'll be with me for ever.'

CHAPTER FIVE

Alone in the morning-room, after they'd left, Abigail felt her whole world crash round her. Marc wouldn't do this to me. He isn't a callous man. It has to be Miranda. Not content with taking my husband, now she wants my child.

But Flora is mine, no-one can take her away from me, Abigail raged.

Yet, like a tiny, stinging insect boring into her, doubt was there. Every word Miranda said was true. They could provide a much better life for Flora, and the child loved and missed her father.

Would she miss me as much, Abigail wondered.

Throwing herself into one of the fireside chairs, she drew her knees up to her chin and wrapped her arms round them. Heat from the smouldering logs warmed her skin. Through the diamond-paned window she saw the sky had turned grey and leaden, making it like twilight, and yet it was only midday. Frost, unmelted, covered the lawn.

At this end of the house, there was silence. Abigail wondered if decorating the Christmas tree was finished. She wanted to go home, back to the two-bedroomed, little terrace house with its handkerchief-sized scrap of garden that Miranda so scorned. There she and Flora would be safe, together. So what's to stop us, she thought, uncurling from the chair.

Back in her bedroom, she began to drag open drawers, grabbing armfuls of clothes, stuffing them haphazardly into her suitcase. Then she would have to find Flora.

The hall was empty when she reached the top of the long, curving staircase and carried her case down. Leaving it near the front door, she ran along the corridor to the drawing-room. Inside, she could hear shrill, excited voices and cautiously opened the door. Flora was handing up a string of tinsel to Luke, who stood on the step-ladder. Abigail went across and took her hand.

'I need you for a moment, sweetheart.'

'Mummy!' the little girl protested. 'I'm helping.'

'Flora!'

Anxiety made Abigail's tone harsh.

'Don't argue.'

'You can come back later to help, Flora,' Luke said, smiling down at her from the top of the ladder. 'Look, we'll save that box of glass birds for you to do.'

'Promise?'

'I promise,' he said.

Pouting, Flora followed Abigail who, stopping only to collect their cagoules and wellingtons from the deserted lobby, carried the suitcase out to her car.

'Where are we going, Mummy?'

Abigail didn't reply, but quickly fastened the seat-belt round her daughter, scraped frost from the windscreen, climbed into the front seat and switched on the engine. It was reluctant to start and Abigail's panic grew as she tried again. With a cough, it finally sprang into life. Abigail pressed down on the clutch pedal and the car moved forward in a series of jerks.

Along the drive they crawled, out through the gates and then they were in the lane, its high banks white with frost. Abigail glanced at the petrol gauge and sucked in her breath. It was almost on empty. She'd need to fill up soon before they went too far. At the back of her mind she recalled passing a garage about a mile or so along the main road on their journey the previous afternoon.

From the rear seat, Flora let out a shriek. Startled, Abigail swung the car away from the grass bank, as she almost drove into it.

'Where's Blue Bun, Mummy? Have you left him behind?'

'I expect he's in the suitcase,' Abigail lied, remembering she hadn't packed him. 'We'll find him later.'

In the distance, she could see the garage and her shoulders relaxed. Once the car was filled with petrol, her worries would be over. It didn't matter how long the journey took, and at home, they would be safe, for a while at least, from Marc and Miranda.

The garage forecourt was blocked by a large, chalked sign. Abigail read it, hardly believing the words.

CLOSED FROM MIDDAY CHRISTMAS EVE UNTIL DECEMBER 26.

Pulling up her sleeve, she looked at her watch. Twenty minutes past twelve!

The place was deserted, no lights anywhere.

Oh, why didn't I fill up the car when I came past yesterday, she fumed, just because it was getting late and I knew Great-Aunt Holly was expecting us for tea. Now, there was no other choice. She reversed the car and began to drive back along the road she'd come.

Somewhere, deep in the house, a gong was

sounding as they slipped into the house through the lobby door. Flora ran off to find the box of glass birds, while Abigail crept up the stairs to their bedroom. There, she sank down on the bed, desperate to know what to do.

'Abigail!'

Someone knocked on her bedroom door.

'Abigail, are you in there? Holly sent me up to find you. It's lunchtime.'

She recognised Luke's voice. Reluctantly, she walked to the door and opened it.

'What's wrong? You've been crying.'

Brushing a hand across her face, she bit her lower lip, trying to steady her mouth before she replied.

'It's nothing.'

He moved into the room and tilted her chin.

'Nothing?'

She saw his gaze rest on the suitcase.

'Do you want to tell me?' he asked, and the concern in his voice made her mouth quiver again.

Abigail shook her head.

'Quite sure?'

She nodded, not daring to say anything in case she broke down completely.

'Then I suggest you give your face a quick wash and come downstairs to lunch. Holly won't let anyone start eating until you're there. You know what a stickler she is for formality.'

He opened the door behind him.

'I'll wait outside for you.'

Abigail wanted to refuse, of course, but Luke's tone didn't allow that. With a deep sigh, she went into the adjoining bathroom and turned on the cold tap.

Abigail was glad Luke was with her as she walked into the dining-room. Without his hand gripping her elbow, she would have turned tail and gone.

'I'm sorry to be so late,' she apologised, fixing her gaze on Great-Aunt Holly.

'My fault, I'm afraid, Holly,' Luke said, steering Abigail towards two empty chairs. 'I shouldn't have taken her down to the beach so early this morning in the freezing cold. She was fast asleep when I went up to find her just now.'

Abigail could tell from the look her great-aunt gave her that she didn't believe Luke, but, tactfully, the old lady said nothing, just inclined her head regally.

'William, will you say grace?' she rapped out.

All those who'd picked up their spoons and were dipping into their soup paused guiltily until William's strong voice had finished blessing the food, then they all began to eat.

'Thank you,' Abigail murmured to Luke, 'for lying about me.'

'It's OK,' he said, and she saw the corners of his mouth twitch. 'I did have my fingers crossed, though!'

Without counting, Abigail decided there must be at least twenty people, including half a dozen children, seated at the long, polished table. It would be easy enough to lose herself among them and avoid Marc and his future wife.

Flora, she noticed with a twinge of pain, was sitting between them, chattering excitedly to her father. Miranda caught her staring and Abigail saw the triumphant twist of her beautiful mouth.

As the meal drew to an end, Great-Aunt Holly tapped on the table with the silver handle of her walking-stick and rose to her feet.

'Now, my dears, I'll tell you the schedule for the rest of the day.'

Immediately, everyone sat up straight in their chairs. Great-Aunt Holly's voice was such that it was an automatic reaction.

'I dare say you all have a few presents left to wrap. When you've done that, please place them under the tree in the drawing-room. After tea, the vicar and his choir are calling in round six o'clock for carols. The children will have a light supper and can watch the Disney film on television until they go to bed.'

She stared hard at one of them, a small boy who was rolling a triangle of cream cheese round the edges of his plate. Sensing her disapproval, he looked up, and popped the triangle into his mouth.

'I'm sure your cheese is quite soft enough, Henry, without the necessity of doing that to it.'

With her mouth in a straight line, she continued.

'Dinner will be at seven o'clock sharp as friends will be joining us for drinks at nine o'clock. Those who wish to may attend the midnight service. I suggest you leave around eleven-thirty.'

'So now we know,' Luke murmured softly. 'Oh, and by the way, Abigail, in case you're set on escaping, there's heavy snow farther up country.'

'Snow?'

He drained his coffee cup and replaced it on the saucer.

'Yes, it was on the news. Blizzards have blocked most of the motorways from the Midlands down into parts of Dorset. They'll probably reach Devon and Cornwall later tonight.'

Pushing back his chair, he stood up.

'So it looks as if we're in for a traditional white Christmas.'

'Oh, no!'

'Are you really so desperate to leave?' he asked gently.

She hesitated, not knowing whether to confide in him or not, yet desperate to talk to someone about what had happened.

'You don't have to tell me anything if you

don't want to, Abigail, but it might help a bit.'

Flora came running up, seized Abigail around the waist, and began to babble excitedly.

'Eleanor, that's the big girl over there with lovely long hair, says there's lots of toys and things upstairs. May I go with the other children to play with them? Eleanor says there's a rocking-horse as big as a real one.'

'Of course you can, darling,' Abigail replied, relieved that the little girl had detached herself from Marc and Miranda. 'Off you go then.'

'Are you too exhausted for another walk before it gets dark?' Luke asked, holding open the dining-room door for her. 'That bitter wind seems to have eased off a little. It often gets warmer before snow comes.'

Abigail looked at him, liking his smile.

'OK, I'll see if I can find that sheepskin jacket again.'

Luke was right, she decided as they stepped out into the crisp air. The wind had ceased, but the sky was very dark now. Without Flora they could walk much faster and the gravel path crunched as they hurried over it, down towards the sea.

'Does it ever freeze?' Abigail asked, clutching at Luke's sleeve when her feet slid on the loose stones.

'The sea, you mean? I've never seen it. It would need to be pretty cold for that to happen, I should think.'

33

He tucked her gloved hand under his arm as he spoke, and she was glad to lean against him as the path became steeper.

'So what was all the panic about this morning?' he queried, holding up a branch as they passed under it.

'My ex-husband and his future wife, Marc and Miranda, want custody of Flora,' she explained. 'Apparently they're getting married early in the new year and . . .'

Her voice quavered slightly before she hurried on.

'And they can provide a secure family and a home for her,' she said, keeping a grip on her emotions.

'Are they allowed to do that, legally, I mean?' Luke asked.

'I don't know,' Abigail said. 'Being down here and with Christmas and everywhere closed for days, there's no way I can consult my solicitor to find out what the truth of the matter is.'

Luke squeezed her arm into his side.

'Marc and Miranda can't do anything either, Abigail. They're in exactly the same boat, stuck here.'

'Miranda's probably researched all the details already. Oh, why did they have to be here, too? At least I could have enjoyed Christmas with Flora, without knowing, until we went home again. Miranda took such pleasure in telling me.'

34

Her body stiffened and she stopped in the middle of the path to stare up at Luke.

'You said you are William's grandson, didn't you? You're not Miranda's brother, are you?'

'No way! She's a cousin. We haven't met up for years. I didn't even know she was getting married. So Marc is your ex-husband? What on earth were my grandfather and Holly doing, having you all here together?'

'My great-aunt was just as horrified as I was,' Abigail explained. 'She had no idea.'

Luke slowed.

'Mind where you step. We're almost at the beach.'

She could hear the sea now. The tide had gone out, but she could just make out the white edge of waves cream over the sand in the half-light. Fine spray blew icily over her face, drifting from the cliffs. Somewhere a lone seabird called. It was a melancholy, haunting sound.

'It's beautiful here in the moonlight,' Luke said quietly, 'but not tonight.'

His arm curved round her shoulders, turning her back towards the path. Briefly, their cheeks touched, and Abigail jerked sharply away as if her skin had been burned.

CHAPTER SIX

Abigail couldn't believe what she'd done. Just a casual brush of cheek against cheek and she'd reacted as though Luke had actually kissed her. It was too dark to see his face, but she'd wondered if he'd even noticed. Silently, they continued on up the path, their breath curling in faint wisps as it met the cold air.

It puzzled her that Luke was here on his own. She remembered their conversation over breakfast after he'd averted a tantrum from Flora.

'You obviously have children of your own,' she'd said.

And he'd replied, 'Quite a few.'

Maybe he and his family live abroad, she thought, and Great-Aunt Holly's demand that everyone be present for her extremely important announcement, which obviously included William's family as well, meant travelling with several children was out of the question.

'Penny for them,' he said, jolting her back to reality.

Abigail laughed.

'For my thoughts?'

'You were miles away. Are you still worrying about Marc and Miranda?'

'No, but you were right, Luke, when you

said there's not much any of us can do until after the Christmas break, so I'll put it all out of my mind for now.'

Her foot slipped on an icy patch and Luke caught her elbow to steady her.

'To be honest, I was wondering where you live and why you're here alone.'

She heard him laugh.

'I live not all that far away, seven or eight miles along the coast. It's a small, fishing village, or was, before all the new rules and regulations made it almost impossible for fishermen to make a living.'

So that explains it, Abigail thought. He'll probably return home tonight and bring his family over to join everyone for Christmas Day, tomorrow. Yet he was here for breakfast this morning, she recalled, and when we were all introduced last night. That's how he knew my name.

I expect he objects to all my questions, which is why he's being so vague. I'll just have to wait and see, she decided.

'How long have your grandfather and my great-aunt been an item, as she puts it?' she asked, stopping for breath as they reached the steepest part of the path.

'As long as I can remember. He was widowed in his late sixties. Holly and my grandmother had been great friends for years. Are you OK to go on now?'

Abigail nodded and they started to walk

again.

'Gran's death from a heart attack came as a great shock to my grandfather, to all of us, in fact. She was always so fit. It upset Holly very much, too. Grandfather used to come here for the occasional meal. I think Holly worried he wasn't looking after himself, which was true. And, gradually, he became a permanent fixture!'

'I love the way my great-aunt calls them an item. Do you think she knows what the term means?'

Luke laughed again.

'Holly's a very up-to-date lady. I'm sure she does.'

'She told me that falling in love wasn't reserved for the young,' Abigail said.

'I don't doubt it can happen any time, anywhere, and to anyone, whatever their age, Abigail.'

He opened the lobby door for her to step inside.

'It's a very comforting thought though, isn't it?'

'Do you think her extremely important announcement is about them, Luke, that they're getting married?'

He unbuttoned his jacket and hung it on one of the pegs, then turned round to face Abigail.

'That seems to be the general opinion, I believe, but we can't be sure. Now, do you need a hand pulling off those wellies?'

'Thanks.'

Abigail raised one leg and watched as Luke bent to tug off the wet boot. He was so different from Marc, untidy in an attractive way, with his faded jeans and well-worn navy sweatshirt. One half of the collar of his check shirt was tucked inside the neck and Abigail felt tempted to straighten it. Without his trainers, she could see a small hole growing in the toe of one thick knitted grey sock, and wondered if it had happened as they walked.

Even though late in the year, his skin was deeply suntanned, as though he spent a lot of time outdoors. Maybe he goes surfing, she decided. In this part of the country it was a popular sport.

Luke stood up.

'There you go. I'll stand them over here to dry off and you can hang your jacket on the peg above, ready for next time.'

Next time? Abigail wondered if there would be a next time. After the Christmas celebrations tomorrow, she'd be taking Flora home, of that she was certain.

'I've still a few presents to wrap, so I'll see you later at tea. In this house, Holly believes one should never stop eating!' he said.

Slowly, Abigail undid her sheepskin jacket and hung it where Luke suggested. Slipping on her trainers, she was tying the laces when she heard the lobby door open behind her.

'I've been searching for you everywhere. We need to talk.'

Abigail didn't look up. She knew exactly who it was.

'I don't think there is anything left to talk about, Marc.'

'Please, Abby. There's so much to explain.'

'I doubt it,' she replied and her tone was acid. 'Everything seems clear to me. Congratulations on your forthcoming marriage, by the way. Don't expect me to be there, throwing confetti though. When is the happy day?'

'January first, but, Abby, it doesn't have to happen.'

His hand moved to touch her cheek and she was very aware of his closeness.

'I still love you, Abby. Seeing you again, after all these months, makes me realise just what I'm giving up.'

Abigail jerked her head away.

'Love me!' she raged. 'How can you say such a thing after all you've put me through? You destroyed everything. I thought we were such a perfect family, you, Flora and me. And then she came along, and you didn't think twice about leaving.'

Marc gripped her shoulders and pulled her towards him.

'You make me sound so callous, but it wasn't like that.'

'What was it like then?'

'You'd been so wrapped up in Flora ever since she was born. I felt left out, Abby, neglected. Life was so different before we had her. You must admit that.'

He ran his fingers down her cheek and a shiver of pleasure filled her whole body.

'Remember what it was like then? Shows, parties, lots of friends, and when we came home . . .'

One finger stroked the corner of her mouth gently and traced the outline of her lips.

'Remember our special moments, Abby?' he whispered softly, leaning towards her.

Abruptly, she pushed him away with a strength that surprised them both.

'Maybe you should have remembered all that,' she replied.

He sat down beside her on the bench.

'I was working with Miranda all day, every day. She was so different from the person you'd become, Abby, beautiful, attractive, lively.'

Abigail glared into his eyes.

'And available,' she said bitterly.

'And available,' he agreed. 'But everything has changed now, Abby. Flora is growing up. You don't have to devote every hour of the day to her any more. We can start again, be a family.'

Fiercely, he put both his arms round her, pulling her against his body.

'I want you, Abby. I want you now.'

41

His mouth closed over hers. For a moment all the old memories, all the old feelings swept over her, and her lips parted. Everything could be like it used to be—until the next beautiful woman came along.

Wrenching her mouth from his, she forced him away.

'Abby, what's wrong?'

His eyes looked into hers, perplexed.

'You're marrying Miranda on New Year's Day, and as far as I'm concerned, she's welcome to you!'

Almost tripping over her laces, Abigail ran from the lobby, down the corridor and up the staircase, into the safety of her room.

The gong, summoning them all for tea, would boom out any minute. There was no way she could go down. No way she could face Marc, or Miranda. How could he say he still loved her, that they could be a family again?

But if I agree, Abigail realised with growing horror, there wouldn't be any chance of losing Flora.

Her first instinct was to go back downstairs, find Marc and tell him she'd made a mistake, that, yes, she did love him, she would go back to him, agree to anything, rather than losing her daughter.

How could I live a lie, though? And it would be a lie, because in that short time alone with him, hearing what he said, and did, I know that I can never love him again. The realisation

42

came as a complete surprise.

For so long she'd clung on to the memory of her love for him, yet now it was gone. It was as though she'd been reborn, seeing clearly what Marc was truly like, her vision unblurred by her feelings for him.

In the hall, the gong sounded. Abigail brushed back her hair, slicked on lipstick, slipped on her shoes, and went down for tea.

The drawing-room, with its tree, looked beautiful. Swathes of holly and ivy decorated the walls and along the top of the fireplace, where logs blazed. A soft scent of pine filled the air.

Flora sat on the floor in the middle of all the children, chattering happily, her cheeks bright with colour. Seeing her mother, she waved and gave a broad smile of happiness.

From the depths of a red velvet sofa, Luke raised his eyebrows in greeting and patted the space next to him, beckoning her over to join him.

At six o'clock, the vicar and his choir would be with them, singing carols. William and Great-Aunt Holly's friends would arrive later. Tomorrow was Christmas Day and suddenly, Abigail told herself, she wasn't going to worry about anything, just enjoy everything while she had the opportunity. After that . . .

She pushed the thought away.

There was a new year coming and with it, she knew, changes that would mean her life would never be the same again.

CHAPTER SEVEN

Abigail didn't go to the midnight service, guessing Flora would be awake very early to discover the contents of her Christmas stocking. Also, if she intended to leave on Boxing Day, she needed to be fresh for that.

Great-Aunt Holly had announced during dinner that stockings could be opened in their bedrooms, but all presents under the tree would wait until after lunch.

'Breakfast will be promptly at eight-thirty,' she said. 'And everyone is expected to join the family service in church at ten o'clock.'

Abigail hadn't been wrong—Flora's excited shrieks when she found her filled stocking woke her just before six and it hadn't been easy to keep her in the bedroom until breakfast time arrived.

The first flakes of snow were drifting down when the family party gathered on the drive ready for church. A few decided to walk through the woods, and others, who were taking their cars, promised to bring back anyone too tired to make the return journey on foot.

Flora, her face hardly visible in the folds of her scarf, wanted to walk with her new friend,

Eleanor, and together they were skipping ahead.

'Wait for me, darling,' Abigail called out anxiously. 'You might get lost.'

'Don't worry so much, Abigail. Eleanor is a sensible child and she knows the way.'

Falling into step beside her, Luke began to follow the others who were striding briskly towards the trees.

'Is it far?' Abigail asked.

'This way it's about half a mile. By road, it's two. We'll be there in ten minutes or so. You'd better hang on to my arm. The path's very uneven.'

With the snow beginning to fall faster, someone leading the way began to sing Good King Wenceslas and the rest chimed in. Looking behind her, Abigail was glad to see that Marc and Miranda were nowhere in sight. They were probably driving there. Miranda's delicate footwear wouldn't cope with a flurry of snow.

The flakes were actually getting larger, swirling down so fast that it was difficult to see the rest of the party, a few metres ahead. The church, when they reached it, came as a complete surprise. Abigail was talking so much to Luke that she scarcely noticed the path through the woods had ended until the force of the wind caught her scarf, twisting it away from her neck and up round her face.

They were almost on the beach and she

could hear waves thud against the rocks, sending spray high into the air to merge with the snowflakes. Luke guided her past the bare, straggling branches of a hedge and through an open, rusting wrought-iron gate almost lost in it, and there, right on the beach, so low it seemed to crouch among high sand-dunes, was the church. It was very old, built of grey, lichened granite, with its bell-tower set beside it as if to make quite sure it was completely hidden.

Brushing snow from their shoulders, the congregation hurried through the heavy, wooden door, anxious to reach the warmth inside. Even Abigail had to bend her head under the arched stone as she went into the tiny porch.

Candles flickered everywhere, their flames quivering or flared high every now and then, giving the interior a soft, ethereal light. Abigail could smell a mixture of matting wax mingled with the slight sootiness of smoke.

Most of the pews were already full, everyone crammed close to make space for others. Luke steered Abigail into one pew beside a thick, round pillar and she tried to read the strange words carved into its depth.

'It's the Lord's Prayer, in Cornish,' he whispered, noticed her interested gaze.

Great-Aunt Holly and William were in the front pew, and beside them she could just see Flora, wedged tightly between them, and

Eleanor. She smiled and waved as Flora turned her head to grin down the aisle at her. A pile of metal chairs was being unstacked now to seat those still coming in through the open door.

Luke edged closer when two more people squeezed into the pew, his thigh firm against hers. Tight against the stone pillar, there was no way Abigail could move away, and was surprised she didn't want to. How anyone would be able to stand for the hymns, she couldn't imagine.

The sound of the organ grew, the notes rising until they seemed to reach the curved rafters of the roof, and the paved floor vibrated. Abigail drew in a deep breath. Christmas Day had really begun.

The vicar gave a very brief sermon, then came down from his pulpit and smiled at the congregation.

'We now have a most unexpected, but delightful event. Never, during a Christmas service, have I been asked to perform such a ceremony but, of course, as you all know, there's a first time for everything.'

In a soft whisper of voices people turned to each other, curious to know what was about to happen.

'Holly, William, come forward, please.'

Abigail watched as her great-aunt and William stepped out of their pew, followed by Flora and Eleanor. The girls, she noticed,

47

were each carrying a small posy of red roses and Great-Aunt Holly was holding a single white rose.

'Now, my dears, let us begin.'

The vicar lifted his head.

'Dearly beloved, we are gathered here this morning to join together this man and this woman . . .'

Pleasure rippled through Abigail. This, she realised, was a wedding ceremony, the reason they were all here now explained. Great-Aunt Holly and William were getting married! She turned to Luke and saw he was smiling back at her.

Abigail had been to many weddings, but not one as perfect as this. Holly and William stood, hands just touching, their gazes fixed on each other with such obvious devotion that Abigail felt tears brim in her eyes. Her great-aunt was right—love wasn't reserved merely for the young.

What else did she say? You can fall in love at any age, Abigail recalled. Well, this was certainly proof of that.

There was a long pause while William struggled to slip the ring over Holly's arthritic finger until, with a smile, she lifted her hand and pushed it on herself. While they were in the vestry signing the register, the choir sang Love Came Down At Christmas and gave new meaning to the carol.

Once again, the organ roared into life, this

time with a triumphant rendering of the Wedding March and the bride and groom stepped confidently down the aisle. Inside the outer room, warmed by a large convector heater, they accepted the congratulations of the congregation as they passed. Abigail and Luke were almost the last to leave.

'Well, Great-Aunt,' Abigail said, kissing her, 'that certainly was a surprise.'

Like a pair of mischievous children, Holly and William looked at each other and laughed.

'I've been wanting to make an honest woman of her for long enough,' William said, with a chuckle.

'Only he was too arthritic to go down on one knee,' Holly replied dryly.

'Why such a secret?' Luke asked.

Holly's mouth tightened.

'Oh, I knew some of the family would try to put us off, getting married at our age. Not quite the thing, is it?'

Luke bent his head to kiss her cheek.

'Well, now the deed is done, so all the luck in the world to you both,' he said in all sincerity.

Having shaken the vicar's hand, Luke and Abigail stepped outside to find it had been snowing steadily for over an hour and the path had completely vanished. Even some of the tombstones were part-buried, where it had drifted against them in the wind, and the hedge curved as if it was made of meringue.

'At least someone's been clearing the track a little so their car can get up to the gate,' Abigail said. 'The poor dears would freeze walking back to the carpark otherwise.'

CHAPTER EIGHT

The carpark was about one hundred metres away, next to a farm where cattle stood in the yard, their breath drifting into steam, as they watched people wade through the snow.

'Walk or ride?' Luke asked as Abigail tried to tie the long ends of her scarf more firmly round her head.

She hesitated. Her feet were already wet from where snow had slid into her boots. Around her, drivers were clearing their windscreens, or trying to open car doors. It was a steep road back. A tractor chugged out of the farmyard, leaving wide black tracks, spoiling the whiteness as it climbed the hill. Behind it followed the bridal car, very slowly. The journey would take a long time.

'Walk,' she said decisively. 'Where's Flora? Has she gone with my great-aunt in the car?'

'No, she's way ahead with Eleanor and her little brother, Henry. The snow is over the top of their boots, but don't spoil it for them. They're having an unforgettable day.'

Hearing the laughter in Luke's voice,

50

Abigail looked up at him. Anyone else would be fussing, saying the snow was far too deep and insisting they went back in one of the cars, but all Luke could see was the children's pleasure.

'We'll rig up some sledges this afternoon, Abigail. I doubt the snow will last very long, so they might as well enjoy it while it's here.'

He caught hold of her hand and began to tug her along.

'There are probably some old trays tucked away in one of the kitchen cupboards. They'll do fine.'

'You're just like a child yourself, Luke.'

'And why not? Childhood doesn't last very long, especially nowadays. It's nice to revert back sometimes.'

A sudden flurry of snowballs hit them when they reached the wood, followed by peals of laughter as the three children jumped out from behind one of the snow-covered bushes.

'Right, young Henry!' Luke roared, gathering up handfuls and pelting them back.

'That's not fair, Uncle Luke!' the little boy shrieked as one landed on the back of his anorak. 'It wasn't my idea. Elly told us to throw them.'

'She did, did she? Come on then, Abigail, two against three is quite fair,' Luke declared.

'But you're bigger than us,' Henry protested.

'And so old we can't run as fast,' Luke told

him.

*   *   *

By the time they reached the house, they were all soaked, but very warm, and had hardly noticed the steep climb back through the wood. None of the cars had arrived.

In the lobby, Abigail struggled to reach behind her head for the knotted ends of her scarf.

'Let me,' Luke said, his hands closing over hers. 'You're only knotting it more tightly.'

Abigail stood quite still as he bent close, feeling his breath warm on her cheek, and her heartbeat quickened.

'There, that's done it.'

Slowly, he unwrapped the scarf from around her face, his fingers brushing her skin, and she found it impossible to turn her head away when they stayed there for an all-too-brief moment.

'What shall we do with our wet clothes and things?'

Flora's voice broke the spell.

'Put them near the central heating pipes, sweetheart,' Abigail replied and was surprised by the unsteadiness of her tone.

'And our boots?' Henry questioned, tipping out melted snow on to the floor.

'Not too close to the heater,' Luke warned.

'Come on then, poppet,' Abigail said swiftly.

'We need a hot shower and to change into our best clothes. I expect Christmas lunch will be a wedding feast now.'

Taking her daughter's hand, she led the way.

'And afterwards,' Henry yelled, stomping along behind them, 'don't forget, it's the presents!'

Later, as she dried Flora's long hair, Abigail realised she hadn't seen Marc and Miranda all morning.

They hadn't been in church and she wondered why. Great-Aunt Holly wouldn't think much of that, especially as the famous surprise had turned out to be her wedding.

So where were they?

CHAPTER NINE

Through the bedroom window, Abigail saw the first car creep up the drive and stop. Snow was still falling heavily and even though someone had brushed it from the front steps, they were already covered again.

One of the staff, holding a large black umbrella, came cautiously down to open the car door and help William, then Holly, out. Abigail heard their voices, but not what they were saying as they hurried into the house.

'Are you ready, Flora? Everyone is coming

back,' she asked her daughter.

'Will it be lunch soon?' the little girl wailed. 'I'm so hungry.'

Abigail laughed as she smoothed her daughter's hair into place.

'What about all those chocolate coins and that very large orange you've eaten since we came home?'

Glancing in the mirror as she tied a long gauze scarf loosely under the collar of her cream silk blouse and straightened the waist of her black velvet skirt, Abigail was surprised to see her face flushed with colour. It had been all that walking through the snow, she decided, refusing to let herself think of Luke.

From the chatter of voices and cold draught in the hallway as she and Flora started to come down the stairs, Abigail knew the rest of the family party had returned. It would be a while before they were all changed ready for lunch, so she led her daughter into the drawing-room to wait.

The room was filled with a glorious smell of pine and wood smoke when she opened the door, the tree lit by a myriad of tiny lights that twinkled on and off.

Flora ran across to look at it, while Abigail sank into one of the deep sofas by the fire and let herself relax. Every now and then a log settled, sending a shower of sparks racing up the chimney as it flared. Some were caught in the soot at the back of the chimney, wavering and glowing, before they finally faded.

Abigail smiled, suddenly reminded of how her grandmother used to say the sparks were people going to church and the last one was the parson, arriving late. It was strange how something could trigger off a long-forgotten memory like that.

'Penny for them.'

Luke's voice startled her. She hadn't noticed him sitting in a high-backed chair at the far side of the room, reading a magazine.

'My thoughts?' she said. 'Oh, not worth a penny, I'm afraid. Just old memories.'

'Nice ones though, from the expression on your face.'

'Yes,' she said, 'but then, old memories usually are. This room is so quiet and peaceful, it seems to produce them.'

'Not for long though,' Luke replied wryly as the door was flung open and some of the children raced in. 'Careful, Henry!' he warned, catching the little boy round the waist and hauling him away from the enormous piles of beautifully-wrapped presents that spread all over the floor under the splendid tree.

'But I want to see what's for me, Uncle Luke.'

'Not until after lunch, that's what Great-Great-Aunt Holly said,' Flora reminded him.

'I'm so excited, I just can't wait that long.'

'Well, you'll have to, Henry, just like everyone else. Listen, that's the gong.'

Luke tightened his hold on the boy.

'Remember your manners, Henry. It's ladies first.'

The dining-room looked magnificent. The polished table had been extended and was decorated with bowls of scarlet carnations and trails of ivy and holly. Candles glowed down its length, highlighting the gleam of silver cutlery and glasses.

Beside each place setting, fat crackers lay, waiting to be pulled. Every child pounced as they sat down, shaking them and peering inside to see what goodies they hid.

Holly and William were already standing, side by side, at one end of the table, and greeted everyone with a kiss as they came in. After searching for her place name, Abigail found she was sitting next to Luke, but seeing the questioning look Holly gave him, wondered if he had changed the cards. Marc and Miranda, she noticed, were seated near the far end and she wondered again where they'd been all morning.

It was a meal Abigail would never forget, and not just for the company she was with. Every course was perfect and the choice far better than a high-class hotel. Holly and William had brought in caterers to combine their wedding feast with a traditional Christmas dinner, but the family atmosphere was retained.

By the time everyone had finished eating, it

was late in the afternoon. The heavy velvet curtains had been drawn when snow clouds made the sky darken early on, enhancing the festive atmosphere by letting them eat by candlelight.

Now, with the children growing more and more impatient as the grown-ups lingered over cheese and biscuits, Holly announced that coffee would be taken in the lounge.

'And,' she added, smiling at the small, anxious faces gazing at her, 'you can all open your presents.'

With whoops of delight, chairs were pushed back, some overturning in the rush to leave the room. Abigail couldn't believe that her usually shy little daughter was leading the mob, even elbowing others out of the way.

More logs were thrown on the fire, popping and crackling, and the huge room was soon filled with shrieks of excitement and the frantic ripping of wrapping paper.

'So much for your peace and quiet, Abigail,' Luke said, balancing a cup of coffee in each hand as he came to sit on the arm of her chair. 'Is this all right for you or would you like more cream?'

'No, it's fine,' she said, taking one of the cups and sipping it. 'But shouldn't you be going home by now?'

Luke raised one eyebrow.

'Well, it is Christmas,' Abigail continued, puzzled. 'What about your children?'

'Oh, I'm quite sure they'll all be enjoying themselves,' he replied, smiling at her. 'More coffee?'

Taking her cup, he moved across the room to where the housekeeper was in charge of several silver jugs.

What a strange man, Abigail thought, watching him. Why does he spend time here when he has a family of his own? Then she had a guess at the reason—he was divorced and the children were with their mother.

'Mummy, Mummy! Look what Daddy's given me!'

Flora ran towards her, holding a doll almost as big as she was.

'If you press this bit, she talks and she can walk, too. See! Miranda has given me loads and loads of clothes for her to wear. Isn't she beautiful? I'm going to call her Eleanor, like my new friend.'

With a twist of resentment gnawing at her, Abigail looked at the doll. It was no comparison with the Barbie she had bought for her daughter, something Flora had been so eager to possess when they saw it in a magazine. Now it was already forgotten somewhere in the growing pile of torn paper.

Looking across to where Marc and Miranda sat closely entwined in a deep armchair, she saw a broad smile curve Miranda's mouth as their gaze met. She stood up and almost ran out of the room.

Upstairs in her bedroom, she let the tears flow. Children are so easily won over. Why should Flora be any different? No wonder she wanted to be with her daddy.

Someone tapped on her door. Abigail sat silent, hoping whoever it was would decide she wasn't there and go away.

'Abigail?'

It was Luke's voice.

'Are you all right?'

The door opened slowly.

'May I come in?'

'You seem to have done that already,' she replied frostily.

'It's just that you looked so upset when you rushed out just now.'

He closed the door quietly behind him and came to sit next to her on the bed.

'What's wrong, Abigail? You were so happy only a short while ago,' he asked tenderly.

She turned her head to look at him. His fingers reached out and gently touched her cheek.

'You're crying. Abigail, please tell me what's wrong.'

'It's no good, Luke. I just can't compete,' she sobbed.

'Compete? What do you mean?'

She wiped the back of her hand across her eyes.

'With Marc and Miranda. Didn't you see that doll? They can give Flora anything she

59

wants, you see. It's so unfair. No wonder she loves them more than me.'

Luke caught hold of her shoulders.

'Of course she doesn't, Abigail.'

'She does, she does.'

The words were lost in a sob of anguish.

'Miranda was right, Luke. Flora would be much happier with them.'

'Is that what you want to happen, Abigail?'

She shook her head.

'Then don't let it. Flora loves you. OK, so she's enjoying being spoiled by Marc. Of course she is. Children are like that. But it's you she loves. You have to fight for her, Abigail.'

'How? They've so much on their side. There's two of them, a mother and father for Flora. They have money and a lovely home. I work, leave Flora with a child-minder, and we live in a shoebox. When it comes to court, who do you think will be chosen as the better parent?'

Pulling her against him, Luke stroked the back of her head and kissed her hair.

'You're Flora's mother, Abigail. There's no question about it. They'll choose you.'

'I only wish I could be sure of that,' Abigail said with a sigh.

Luke stood up and held out his hand.

'Come back downstairs. You haven't opened your presents yet.'

'I haven't got any.'

'Of course you have. Everyone has. Holly wouldn't leave anyone out,' Luke insisted.

Laughter crinkled his eyes.

'There's one from me anyway.'

Abigail frowned.

'You? Why would you give me a Christmas present? You don't even know me.'

'But I want to,' he said quietly, catching hold of her hands and pulling her to her feet.

Momentarily, as she almost lost her balance, their bodies touched, until Abigail jerked backwards, twisting away. Quickly she turned to the dressing-table, picked up a brush and began to sweep it through her hair, but reflected in the mirror she could see very clearly that his eyes registered surprise, and something more.

Refusing to meet his gaze, she wiped away smudged mascara and added more, her hand trembling as she did. Then, taking a deep breath, she stood up and faced him.

'Am I presentable now?'

Laughter lines were deep around his eyes.

'Hmm, let me look at you closely,' he replied, tilting her chin with one finger.

For a moment, she thought he was going to kiss her and her breathing stopped, but his hand dropped away as he said, 'Highly presentable, Abigail. Shall we go down?'

The sound of excited voices echoed along the corridor when they reached the foot of the stairs and the volume increased as Luke opened the drawing-room door. While the grown-ups lolled in a haze of warmth on sofas or in armchairs, some already asleep, others nearly there, the children were scattered round the room, examining their own and each other's presents.

Abigail's eyes searched for Flora. Eleanor, she could see, was helping her brother, Henry, construct a cardboard castle, so Flora must be nearby. She trailed her new friend like a small shadow. Abigail let her gaze scan the room again, her heart pounding, then she untensed a little. Of course, Flora would be with Marc and Miranda, playing with that doll. But where? She turned to Luke.

'Can you see Marc anywhere, or Flora?'

Craning his neck, Luke studied the crowded room, then shook his head.

'Miranda, is she around?' Abigail asked, her breath catching in her throat.

'Don't worry so. They're sure to be somewhere around.'

Flinging open the door, she ran down the corridor to the lobby, tugging at its handle.

'Wait, Abigail. I'll do it.'

Once inside, she paused, then walked slowly to where Flora had left her anorak and boots, knowing, even before she reached it, they wouldn't be there. Luke's fingers gripped her shoulders.

'Don't get so upset, Abigail. They've probably just gone for a walk.'

She glared up at him, her eyes brimming.

'In the dark? In the snow? Don't be so stupid, Luke.'

Her fingers clenched into fists as she pounded them into his chest and her voice rose.

'Marc's taken Flora, Luke, and he has no intention of bringing her back.'

CHAPTER TEN

'Abigail! You're jumping to conclusions,' Luke said calmly, putting his arm round her. 'I can't see Mark taking Flora anywhere on a night like this. Give him some credit, Abigail. After all, he is her father.'

'You really don't understand, do you, Luke? Marc wants Flora and he doesn't care how he sets about it. Going to court will take time. He's not prepared to wait.'

'Please, Abigail, let's just check the house first, shall we?'

Reluctantly, Abigail followed Luke back to the drawing-room and listened while he raised his voice to ask if anyone had seen Flora, Marc or Miranda anywhere.

'I did,' Henry shouted, looking up from constructing a toy castle.

'Where?' Luke said, crouching on his heels beside the little boy.

63

'Well, I didn't exactly see them, but I did hear their car driving away. I saw it was their car because it's a Range Rover like Daddy wants, only he says he can't afford it because he has to feed me and Ellie and Mummy.'

'And do you know where Flora is?' Luke asked patiently.

The little boy nodded.

'She was showing me how that silly doll could talk and then that pretty lady with the golden hair like a princess came to find her. She said there were lots more presents outside in their car and they were all for Flora.'

He glanced up at Luke.

'That wasn't very fair, was it, Uncle Luke? All the presents were supposed to be in here under the tree, weren't they? Anyway, Flora wanted to go and find them, so they went out of the door.'

'Did Flora and Miranda go out before you saw the car drive off, Henry?' Luke went on.

'Yes. Flora was going to help me build my castle but now she's gone and nobody else wants to. Perhaps they're looking for some more presents for me and Ellie, and everyone,' he added as an afterthought.

Luke stood up.

'You're quite sure Flora went with Miranda, Henry?' he persisted.

The little boy was studying another piece of the castle.

'Yes.'

Abigail tugged at Luke's arm.

'We have to go after them, now, before they get too far.'

'But we've no idea which direction they've taken, Abigail. And in this weather . . .'

His voice trailed away.

Holly crossed the room to join them, catching their conversation, and put her arms round Abigail to hug her.

'My dear, do you really think Marc's taken Flora?'

Abigail nodded.

'But we can follow their car tracks,' she said eagerly.

'My dear, that's quite impossible. Look outside. Any tracks will have been completely obliterated within minutes by the snow.'

With her face buried in her great-aunt's shoulder, Abigail's reply was muffled.

'But we have to do something. We can't just sit here. Flora is my child. I want her back.'

'Luke!' Holly ordered. 'Contact the police straight away. They'll be able to check all roads.'

She patted Abigail's cheek.

'Don't worry, my dear, they'll have little Flora back before you know it,' she said comfortingly.

She turned her head.

'Have you got through yet, Luke?'

Replacing the receiver on its base, Luke shook his head.

'The phone is dead, Holly. The snow must have brought down the overhead lines. I'll try my mobile.'

Silently, everyone watched him tap out the digits, and then he shook his head again.

'Nothing. Can I borrow someone else's mobile?'

Hands delved into pockets and handbags, producing a variety of tiny phones, but not one of them functioned.

'The whole area seems to be blanked out,' Luke said, his expression bleak. 'Reception is often very poor or non-existent down this way, but tonight it's quite impossible.'

'So what are we going to do?' Abigail asked, her voice desperate.

'My dear, there's nothing we can do, except wait,' Holly advised.

'Wait!' Abigail snapped out, twisting away from her great-aunt. 'Do you honestly think I'm going to sit here and wait, while Flora . . .'

Her voice broke.

'I know, my dear, I know,' Holly comforted, 'but really, there is nothing else we can do until the morning. By then a thaw could set in. If not, at least in daylight someone might be able to reach the village on foot.'

She glanced round at the worried faces surrounding her.

'Try to be brave, Abigail, my dear. At least Marc can't drive far in this weather. They may even have to return. Now, I think we should all have some tea, always such a help in a situation like this.'

Abigail had never spent such a long night. Every minute dragged as though it were an hour and the snow continued to fall. Just before midnight, when most of the party was still sitting round the blazing wood fire, everything went black.

'Oh, no! This is too much. Now the power's gone,' Holly announced. 'Can someone find the candles? I think they were put on the sideboard after lunch. Just one of you, or there will be confusion.'

'I'll go,' Luke said, and Abigail felt the warmth of him move away from her side, making her shiver.

In the darkness she could see firelight flicker on people's faces, sending long, wavering shadows over the ceiling and walls. No-one spoke. Outside, there was an eerie silence as snow blanketed the walls of the house, muffling every sound. Even the sea was quiet.

Where, oh, where, she groaned inwardly, is Flora? Is Marc's car stuck in a drift somewhere? Has it slid from the road, down a bank, with snow rapidly covering it? Are they injured? Is Flora frightened, needing me there with her? She's never been away from me before. Marc is almost a stranger now, it's been so long since he was with us. And as for Miranda, she is a stranger.

She heard the door open and felt a cold draught as Luke returned. Bending, he lit one red candle, then another, from the glowing fire, and set them in the safety of the brick grate.

'Ah, that's better,' she heard Holly breathe. 'William, dear, will you bring one of those and we'll go and make more tea?'

Abigail's fingers slipped into Luke's and she was comforted as his grip closed firmly round hers.

'Flora will be all right, Abigail,' he whispered, his lips brushing the lobe of her ear. 'Marc will look after her. He'll make sure she's quite safe. Don't worry about that.'

'But if their car gets stuck in a snowdrift, they could freeze.'

His fingers tightened round hers.

'They won't, Abigail. That Range Rover is a big, powerful vehicle. I doubt it could get stuck anywhere. Cars like that are built for extreme conditions, remember.'

Hearing the positive note in his voice, she relaxed a little, letting her head sink into the comfort of his shoulder.

'Where do you think he's taking her, Luke? There's no way they can travel abroad, is there? Being Christmas, all the ferries stop, don't they? Especially in weather like this.'

'I'm not really sure,' he said, resting his chin against her hair. 'They'd probably need to reach Plymouth to catch a ferry in any case, and there's no way they can do that in this snow.'

He paused and, tensing, she lifted her head to look at his face, shadowed in the candlelight.

'What, Luke?'

'There is a small airport at Penzance,' he said reluctantly, then swiftly added, 'But there's no way a plane could take off from there tonight.'

'Are you sure?' she asked doubtfully.

'Quite sure.'

With a faint clinking of china and rattle of wheels over the polished wooden floor, Holly pushed a laden tea-trolley into the room.

'Right then, my dears. Sorry to be so long, but the kettles took a while to boil on the stove. Now, help yourself to a cup of tea. The mince pies are cold, I'm afraid, but the Christmas cake will be quite filling. It's going to be quite a time until breakfast.'

In a rustle of movement, everyone gathered round the trolley, selecting plates of food, before settling back into their chairs again.

'Abigail,' Holly said softly, leaning towards her, 'William mentioned something in the kitchen that I think you should know.'

She nudged his shoulder.

'Well, tell them, dear.'

William balanced his cup and saucer on his lap.

'Not a great deal of information really, but I

69

was talking to Marc over lunch. I asked him where he and Miranda had been all morning, when Holly particularly requested everyone to be in church. Damned rude, I thought, and told him so.'

He picked up the cup and sipped from it, before clattering it back on to the saucer.

'Blustered around for a while, trying to avoid the issue, but I was determined to have an answer.'

'Oh, do get to the point, William!' Holly interrupted.

'I am, Holly, be patient.'

He turned his head to where Abigail was sitting upright, her fingers digging into her palms.

'As I was saying, eventually Marc told me what they'd been doing. No apology, mind you.'

'What had they been doing?' Luke asked quietly, his arm tight round Abigail.

'Checking out their new boat.'

'Boat,' Abigail murmured. 'Oh, no.'

'Bought it a couple of days ago, Marc said. Quite sizeable, from how he described it, powerful motor, too. Apparently that girl of his owns a little place on the coast of Britanny. Said it would have them across there in no time. Wouldn't mind one like that myself.'

With a groan, Abigail twisted round and buried her face into Luke's neck. Smoothing away her tangled hair, he kissed her forehead, his fingers gently trailing a path down the side of her face to tilt her chin.

'Please, don't get so upset, Abigail. There's no way they can go anywhere tonight, and tomorrow, whatever the weather is like, we'll find Flora. I promise.'

CHAPTER ELEVEN

Exhausted by anxiety and tears, combined with the heat from the fire and soothing glow of the candles, Abigail finally fell asleep, curled into Luke's side. Others in the family had crept upstairs as the night wore on, glad to sink into their beds, glad, too, that it wasn't their own child who was missing.

Despite pleading with them to go to bed as well, William and Holly insisted on remaining downstairs, but even they, too, drifted into sleep, cuddled together on one of the sofas. Eventually, even Luke couldn't stay awake . . .

Flora was calling her. Abigail could hear the plaintive, little voice quite clearly, but couldn't find her. Everywhere was white—a dazzling brightness that hurt her eyes, so that she had to close them. But still Flora's cries continued.

The snow was so deep. It was like trying to swim against the tide. Every movement Abigail made forced her backwards, so that she was getting farther and farther away from the sound as it grew fainter.

'Flora!'

The name was torn from her lips.

'Abigail, it's all right. Wake up. You've been dreaming.'

Shivering with cold, Abigail opened her eyes. In the half-light of the room, Luke's weary face, dark with stubble, was gazing down at her. The fire had burned to a pile of grey ash, glowing here and there with sullen colour where flakes of wood still smouldered. One stump of candle flickered in a deep pool of wax.

Yawning, she struggled to sit up.

'Flora?'

Her eyes pleaded with him.

Sadly, Luke shook his head and eased his feet to the floor. Walking stiffly over to the windows, he pulled back one of the velvet curtains. Snow was piled halfway up the glass and frost patterns etched the rest. Abigail couldn't decide whether it had stopped snowing or not.

'What's the time?'

Luke pushed up the sleeve of his sweatshirt.

'Just gone eight.'

'Eight!' she cried, joining him at the window. 'We should have left by now. Why didn't you wake me?'

As she turned, he caught her wrist.

'Wait, Abigail. You must eat first. There's no good rushing off in this cold without food inside you. Go and shower and get dressed in warm clothes. I'll see to some breakfast.'

'But . . .'

Luke placed one finger over her lips.

'No buts, Abigail. Just do as I say.'

By the time she came downstairs again, Luke had two steaming bowls of porridge on the kitchen table and a kettle was whistling faintly on the nearby Aga.

'I'm not hungry,' she murmured, pushing away the bowl.

'Eat!' he commanded, sitting down and beginning to devour his. 'You're going nowhere until you have.'

'What about everyone else?' she asked, picking up her spoon and beginning to eat.

'They can sort themselves out. I've taken some tea in to Holly and William. What a way to spend their wedding night. They seem quite cheerful about it, though.'

'I'm so sorry. They must hate me for ruining all the celebrations,' she said, feeling quite guilty.

'Of course they don't. It's Marc and Miranda who should be sorry, Abigail, not you. Do you want coffee or tea?'

'Coffee, please.'

With the porridge eaten, she wrapped her fingers round the mug, glad of its comforting warmth. Luke, she noticed, was cutting bread and filling it with slices of ham. He saw her watching and smiled.

'Just in case we get stuck in a snow drift,' he explained, wrapping foil round the hefty sandwiches. 'I'll be about five minutes getting showered and changed, then we'll be off. Have you everything?'

'Blue Bun!' Abigail gasped. 'Flora's toy rabbit. She'll be missing him. She never goes anywhere without him.'

Following Luke upstairs, Abigail ran along the corridor to her bedroom and tugged back the covers on Flora's little bed. Blue Bun's threadbare face, one ear crumpled, gazed blankly back at her through brown glass eyes.

Abigail picked him up, kissed his squashed nose, and slipped him into the pocket of her fleece jacket.

She would collect the sheepskin coat and her boots from the lobby on the way out.

Snow had drifted against the back door so that she and Luke had to heave it open, making a gap just wide enough to squeeze through.

Together they struggled across the yard to where white mounds hid the cars.

'William gave me the keys to his Land-Rover. It stands a better chance of getting through than my clapped-out, old banger.'

'But which one is it?' Abigail asked, her eyes scanning the line of buried cars.

Luke grinned at her.

'William keeps his in one of the garages.'

He tugged open a wooden door.

'This one.'

Helping Abigail to climb in, it took him three tries before the engine would start then, with a roar, the vehicle jolted out, pushing the snow away as it did so.

'It's going to be a very slow journey, I'm afraid, Abigail, but at least we're moving.'

Once they'd left the driveway behind and were in the lane, the snow wasn't quite so deep.

The high banks and hedges had sheltered the road a little, but every so often deep drifts stretched across, forcing the Land-Rover to a slithering crawl.

'The main road might not be so bad, if they've had a chance to get the snow ploughs out and gritted them,' Luke commented, peering through a small gap in the windscreen that remained clear.

'And if they have, that means Marc will be way ahead of us,' she replied, her voice wavering. 'There's no chance we'll ever be able to catch him up. Oh, why didn't we leave last night?'

'Don't be such a pessimist, Abigail. You know if we had, with the snow falling, we'd never have got through. At least it's stopped for a while, and it's daylight.'

'But it's pointless, Luke. We've no idea which direction Marc will have taken.'

She saw his mouth curve up at the corners.

'Haven't we, Abigail?'

Hearing the laughter in his voice, she stared at him, her eyes widening.

'William told me when I took in their tea this morning, he remembered what Marc had said about the boat. It's anchored in a little harbour only a few miles from here.'

Luke had been right—a snowplough had cleared the main road. It had taken nearly two hours to reach there, and at times Abigail despaired that the Land-Rover would ever make it when its engine revved uselessly, trying to force a way through.

'It should be a bit easier from now on,' Luke said encouragingly, turning his head to look at her. 'Do you want some hot coffee? I've brought a couple of flasks.'

'Let's leave it until we reach the harbour,' she replied. 'I don't want to waste any more time. Marc had a good start on us.'

'Yes, but don't forget, this road wasn't cleared then. That snowplough has been along here quite recently. There's only a sprinkling of snow covering the road.'

'So they might be only slightly ahead?' she said. 'Do you think they've taken food and something to drink, like you?'

'Hopefully, but they did leave in rather a hurry, didn't they? We weren't away from the lounge for more than half an hour.'

'Oh, don't say that, Luke.'

The idea of little Flora being hungry, as well as frightened, horrified her completely.

'No need to look so worried, Abigail. They were pretty well organised, don't forget, so probably loaded their car earlier. I expect they provisioned the boat when they were down there yesterday, while we were all in church.'

'How much farther is it? How long will it take?'

'The road narrows again after we've skirted the town, and is quite steep in places. It all depends on whether or not there's been a snowplough out on it. If not, it could take quite a while, I'm afraid.'

'But it will be the same for Marc, won't it, Luke?'

He smiled at her.

'Of course it will. And they may have stopped somewhere to eat, if they can find anywhere open on Boxing Day.'

'Should we look?' Abigail asked.

Luke shook his head.

'No, we'll keep going. If we're ahead of them, all the better.'

The road conditions grew worse when they began to climb the winding hill away from the town, and Abigail scanned the sides of the road ahead, dreading to see Marc's vehicle lying somewhere.

CHAPTER TWELVE

It had stopped snowing and a pale halo of sun appeared and disappeared through grey cloud as it thinned. Abigail's head ached from the glare of whiteness hiding the hedges and fields on either side. She wanted to close her eyes to ease them, but dared not, and her fingers clung to the toy rabbit tucked deep into the pocket of the borrowed sheepskin jacket.

Without Blue Bun for comfort, Flora would be distraught. Given as a present for her first birthday, she'd taken him everywhere with her ever since, hugging him so often that his face and fur were almost worn away. None of her other toys had been the same.

Where is she? Abigail agonised. Is she frightened without me there? She loves her daddy, but being snatched away like that—how would Marc and Miranda explain that to her?

'There's the sea.'

Luke's voice broke into her thoughts, and Abigail peered through the spattered windscreen, at first seeing nothing but endless grey. Slowly it turned into a faint haze of sky meeting white-flecked dark sea. Granite-stone houses began to border the wet road.

'Fantastic!' Luke breathed. 'They've gritted the hill down to the harbour. I was worried we'd have to leave the Land-Rover at the top and walk.'

They were passing small shops now, every window dark, but still decked out for Christmas, and Abigail saw the curve of sea wall where the road turned.

'I'll park beside the harbour,' Luke said, and then they were bumping over cobbles until the vehicle skidded slightly as it stopped.

From her high seat, Abigail looked down at grey rippling water enclosed by a horseshoe shape of stone wall. A collection of fishing boats swayed together, their moorings hidden in drifts of snow. The harbourside was deserted. Wiping the mist of her breath from the window, Abigail searched for some sign of life. Two herring gulls flew down to perch on the top of the wall, yellow eyes gazing unblinking at her.

She could hear the faint tap, tap of metal ropes as they rattled against the masts of the boats. Empty lobster or crab pots were stacked against some buildings on the opposite side of the water. Smoke rose, wavering sideways, from nearly every chimney of a straight terrace of houses climbing the hill. Everywhere was silent.

A draught chilled through her as Luke opened the car door and jumped down to lean over the wall. With a squawk of protest the gulls lifted heavy wings and flapped away to settle again on the side of one of the boats, making it sway. Abigail waited, her body tensed, her stomach taut, her nails digging into the handle of the door, not knowing if she ought to join Luke.

She watched him walk along slowly, studying each boat. Then, stamping the snow from his boots, he was back beside her in the Land-Rover. Closing her eyes, she bit down hard on her lower lip, knowing what he would say.

'I'm so sorry, Abigail, but we're too late. They've taken advantage of the break in the weather and already gone.'

CHAPTER THIRTEEN

It took a moment for the full meaning of Luke's words to filter into Abigail's brain. Flora was gone, and she had no idea where. All the time they'd been driving, there was hope, but now there was nothing left. She felt like an empty shell.

'We will get her back, Abigail.'

Through the hollowness she felt, Abigail noticed that Luke said we and that small word gave her comfort. She wasn't alone. Luke was there to help her.

'You need a drink,' he said, putting an arm round her shaking shoulders and mechanically she let him guide her in through the door of a harbourside pub.

Comforting warmth wrapped round her like a blanket as she sank into the depths of a worn leather sofa by an open fireplace. There was a questioning silence when they came in, glasses poised between bar and mouth while heads turned to study them. Then the buzz of conversation started up again to surround her.

She watched Luke as he bent to speak to the barman, and saw a couple of glasses swiftly polished with a cloth before being filled.

'It's brandy,' Luke said, returning, and, guessing the protest she was about to give, continued, 'Just drink it.'

Abigail coughed as the liquid slid down her throat.

'It's far too strong,' she protested.

'Finish it,' Luke ordered, sinking beside her on to the sofa. 'Then I want you to listen.'

Obediently, she screwed up her face and choked down the rest as if it were foul-tasting medicine.

'Good! Sorry to be so brutal, but you'll feel better in a minute or two. You look like death.'

She leaned back against the soft leather and closed her eyes, surprised to find her body relaxing.

'I had a chat with the barman, Abigail. Mentioned we were looking for Marc's boat.'

Luke picked up his glass and drank some of the brandy before continuing.

'Apparently it caused a lot of interest. Not quite the type of vessel they usually see in the harbour. It stood out among the fishing boats, as did Miranda when they were here yesterday morning.'

'She is rather striking,' Abigail murmured.

'You could say that, I suppose. Rather doll-like, I thought. Anyway, the boat was moored over there.'

Luke pointed through the window behind them.

'The barman said it left about an hour or so ago. Didn't see who was on it though.'

Abigail jerked up and struggled with the slippery leather in an effort to sit upright.

'An hour or so! Luke, we have to hire a boat and go after them. They can't be very far out.'

'It's a powerful motor cruiser, Abigail. Just look, there's nothing in this harbour that could ever catch up with that. Besides, the weather is closing in again.'

Rubbing condensation from the glass, Abigail peered out. Even in the few minutes they'd been inside the pub, the sky had grown black, with a few flakes of snow already drifting down, swirling in the rising wind.

White-capped waves pounded in through the wide outer harbour entrance to race along the inside of the sea wall, faster and faster. From the safety of the inner harbour, fishing boats no longer gently rose and fell, but twisted this way and that, tugging at the ropes that moored them, nudging each other like impatient horses.

And Flora was out there somewhere!

The thought tore through her and her fingers smoothed the worn blue fur of the toy rabbit, hidden in her pocket. Abigail bit her lip hard. Crying wouldn't bring her little daughter back.

'She will be all right,' Luke said, but when Abigail looked into his eyes, she read a doubt in them.

The snow was thickening now, hiding the sky, feathering the windows, piling up on the sills as the wind increased. Abigail could no longer see the boats, or even the harbour itself.

Her ears tuned into a group of fishermen standing nearby, gazing out at the weather as they drank their pints.

'No-one gone out today in this, 'ave they, Matthew?'

'Only that posh 'un. He was warned the weather would turn bad again, but that woman hustled him on.'

'Let's 'ope he knows what he's be doing then and turned back. Them Manacles aren't choosy who they takes.'

Puzzled, Abigail turned to Luke.

'What do they mean, manacles?'

Luke hesitated before replying.

'They're rocks, Abigail.'

He stood up.

'I'll go and order some soup. We need something after that brandy.'

'You haven't finished telling me about those rocks.'

With a sigh, he sat down beside her again.

'They're notorious,' he said and his voice was toneless. 'Countless ships have been wrecked on them over the centuries.'

'And still are?' she whispered.

He nodded.

'But we don't know Marc is heading in that direction, Abigail. He could be going anywhere.'

One of the fishermen leaned towards them.

'Any vessel out in a sea like that, with this wind, won't have no choice of direction. Like it or not, 'tis the Manacles he'll be taken to.'

Abigail's nails dug into Luke's palm as her fingers clenched tightly round his.

'Best let coastguard know,' the man continued, turning back to his friends. 'Dare say he'll have the helicopter up.'

But even while he was speaking, a faint splutter of noise like a swarm of bees grew until, with an ear-splitting roar, it was overhead, then receded, on its way out to sea.

'Something must have happened already,' the man said eagerly, zipping up his heavy jacket. 'Best be down on the jetty, lads. Never know what might be brought back.'

Already too numb to take any more emotion, Abigail sat, shaking silently, her face so pale it was almost transparent. Her child's name pulsed inside her with every beat of her heart.

Luke's arms closed round her, holding her close against him, his cheek resting on hers, but there was nothing he could say to comfort her.

A flurry of snow and freezing air swept in through the open door as the group of men went out, slamming it behind them, leaving silence. The barman came across to gather up their empty glasses, pausing for a moment to look down at Abigail's bent head.

'Know someone on that boat, does she?' he asked Luke.

'Her little girl.'

The man flinched and his face changed to sadness.

'Oh, the poor little love.'

Listening to his words, muffled through Luke's arm, Abigail wasn't sure if he meant her or Flora, but felt their kindness.

'I'll bring over some soup. Might be a long wait. Would you like another drink to go with it?'

Luke shook his head and the movement roused Abigail. Wiping her eyes with the back of her hand, she looked into Luke's face.

'Flora will die, won't she? Drowned! She may even be dead already,' she said in a whisper.

Her voice broke and a cascade of tears poured down her cheeks.

'She can swim though. Started when she was

85

a baby. They ran a special class at our local swimming baths. She loved it so much.'

There was a clatter from behind the bar as a round, little woman appeared, carrying a tray.

'There, my dears, you have a little of this and stop fretting. Nothing's ever as bad as you think.'

She put the bowls in front of them, and added a plate of crusty granary bread, pats of butter and serviettes wrapped round spoons and knives.

'The helicopter lads don't give up easily. Such courage and daring, it makes me want to weep sometimes that they can be so brave,' she said in all sincerity.

Fishing out a box of tissues from the pocket of her apron, she put it on Abigail's lap.

'Thought you might need a few of these, 'til your little one's back safe and sound. And she will be, I assure you. I'm never wrong. Ask anyone round this way.'

With a patter of heels on the terracotta floor, she was gone again, back into her kitchen.

'Well, my dears,' the barman called across to them, 'if Nance says everything's going to be all right, it will.'

A tiny surge of hope flickered through Abigail. The little woman had been so positive.

Wiping her cheeks with a tissue, she unrolled the serviette, picked up the spoon

86

and dipped it into the steaming bowl of soup. After looking at her in amazement for a moment, Luke did the same.

They were just coming to the end of the meal, when a glimmer of sound could be heard outside. Abigail's body tensed, her eyes widening with apprehension as the whole building began to vibrate with noise.

'Surely it can't be landing here?' she whispered, staring at Luke.

The thud of boots running over the cobbles stopped outside the pub door, then it was flung open and one of the fishermen hurtled through in a blast of cold air.

'Come on, my dears! Come on!'

Bundling Abigail into her jacket, Luke slipped his arms into his, still zipping it up as they were hustled outside. The snow had stopped, leaving a crisp covering on the ground, marred only by a wavering line of melting footprints.

With Luke and the fisherman each holding her hands, Abigail found herself propelled towards the helicopter, where something wrapped in an orange blanket was being carried out by a shapeless, helmeted figure.

Suddenly, Abigail didn't want to know. Her feet stopped moving, but still she was being dragged on, sliding over the snowy cobbles of the harbour. And then she saw a head appear, pushing its way out through the swathe of blanket.

'Flora!'

Abigail released the hands holding hers and, choking back sobs of relief, slithered and slid towards her child, hugging her tightly as the crewman put the little girl into her arms.

'Strictly against the rules, you know,' he said, with a broad grin. 'But we received a radio message to say her mum was waiting here, so . . .'

He winked.

'Well, some rules are made to be broken, aren't they? We'll catch up with you later. In a bit of a rush. Have to return for one more. Don't worry, she's fine. Just needs her mum.'

'I can never thank you enough,' Abigail breathed, then with Flora's arms tight round her neck, turned and began to trudge back towards the pub, where a growing crowd had started to gather.

'Mummy, Mummy, it was so exciting! All the sea was coming in the boat and Daddy didn't know what to do, and Miranda was being sick everywhere and then . . . guess what?'

'What, darling?'

'This ginormous helicopter came and a man . . . his name was Steve, 'cos he told me . . . came twiddling down on a bit of string, like a spider only he didn't have a web, and . . .'

She gave a great chortle of glee.

'He picked me up and we went twiddling round and round with all the waves trying to get us, right up into the helicopter.'

'And what about Daddy and Miranda?'

'Oh, Steve went back and got Miranda. Daddy stayed to save the boat 'cos Miranda said it cost lots of money.'

Abigail was only half-listening.

'But weren't you frightened, darling?'

Flora twisted her head to look at her mother with surprised eyes.

'No,' she said. 'It was like television, only real. Ellie and Henry are going to be so amazed when I tell them. Are we going home now?'

Back inside the pub, the little girl, cuddling her precious Blue Bun, was fussed over by everyone, but was more anxious about getting back to her new friends than anything else. It was only then that Abigail realised what Flora had said earlier—Daddy stayed to save the boat 'cos Miranda said it cost lots of money.

When the helicopter went back, did it find him? A hopeless feeling of dread swept over her. There could only be one answer.

Their drive home was much quicker, with the snow melting. Already, as so often happens by the sea, the squally wind had died down as quickly as it had come.

Guessing that everything Marc had done was under pressure from Miranda, Abigail cuddled Flora in the joy of knowing that her child was safely back with her again.

CHAPTER FOURTEEN

A terrible feeling of tiredness engulfed Abigail once they were back at the manor house again, a reaction to all that had happened, and grief for Marc. Once, she had loved him, something that would never be forgotten.

'You were on the telly, Flora!' young Henry greeted them in the hallway, jumping up and down with excitement. 'On the news. We saw it, didn't we, Ellie? My daddy said he'd video it if it's on again tonight, then you can watch every day.'

In a hubbub of chatter, the children swept Flora away with them. Abigail wondered if she should make the little girl sleep for a while, but decided it might be better to let the whole episode seem an adventure, rather than the horror story it was, not that the child appeared to regard it as anything but an exciting adventure.

'It's you who needs some rest,' Luke said, easing her out of her heavy jacket. 'You look exhausted.'

'And you must be, too,' she replied, placing a hand either side of his stubbled cheeks. 'All that dreadful driving, and having to cope with me.'

He smiled.

'Every second was worth it to have Flora

safe again.'

'What do you think will happen now?' Abigail asked, letting him guide her up the stairs.

'Marc is dead, Abigail. The boat was matchwood when the helicopter crew went back. It was on the news. Holly told me.'

His arm tightened round her shoulders.

'I'm so sorry, Abigail. As for Miranda, she seems to have been the driving force behind everything. Marc just did whatever she told him. I'm sure the police will sort it all out. She has no claim on Flora anyway.'

Pausing on the landing, Luke turned towards the narrow window.

'Look, the sun's breaking through all that cloud. Maybe tomorrow, if a thaw sets in, the snow drifts will clear from the lanes and I can drive you over to the village where I live.'

He gave her a cautious glance.

'That is, if you'd like to.'

Abigail smiled.

'I'd like to very much.'

And then she remembered, tomorrow she and Flora were returning home.

'The police are sure to need you to stay on for a day or so, until it's all settled,' Luke said, as if reading her thoughts yet again.

'Yes,' she replied slowly. 'They probably will.'

*   *   *

When Abigail woke the following morning, it was to find her bedroom wall patterned with the dancing shadows of trees and the sun shining in through a gap in the curtains. Curled in a tight, little ball, Flora still slept, her small face buried in Blue Bun's fur.

Leaning on one elbow, Abigail gazed across from the four-poster bed. How different this day could have been, she thought.

Her body tensed, seeing in her mind's eye those dark, granite rocks with the sea pounding over them, and Marc's boat, seized by the fierce currents, racing towards them. But Flora was safe, asleep in the bed beside hers, quite oblivious to the horror of what might have been.

Abigail climbed out of bed and stepped into the adjoining bathroom to shower, letting hot, fragrant water swirl away her tortured thoughts. Today, she remembered, Luke was taking her to see his home, and there I'll meet his family.

But Flora wasn't too pleased about the visit.

'I don't want to come, Mummy,' the little girl wailed later over breakfast, when told where they were going. 'Great-Great-Aunt Holly and Uncle William have made a treasure hunt in the house for all the children and Ellie says I can be with her.'

'Well . . .' Abigail said doubtfully.

'You can't let the child miss out on the fun,'

Holly announced briskly.

'Besides, Eleanor is a sensible girl and will look after her, won't you, dear? Now, off you go, Abigail. Don't keep Luke waiting.'

For a moment Abigail hesitated, torn between Flora and Luke, then, seeing him emerge from the lobby, his arms full of jackets and boots, she gave the little girl a kiss and went to meet him.

He'd said the previous day, before they set out to follow Marc, that his car was old. Abigail hadn't realised quite how old though, until she saw him lift the bonnet and remove a tartan rug protecting the engine of an ancient Morris Minor. Then, to her amazement, he produced a starting handle, inserted it somewhere above the number plate and proceeded to heave it round until, finally, a splutter of noise erupted and the whole car began to tremble.

'Quick, Abigail, hop in before she stops again.'

CHAPTER FIFTEEN

Apart from deep snow still covering the sloping banks under the high hedges bordering them, the lanes were clear. As the car gathered speed when it reached the main road, Abigail saw sunshine sparkle the surrounding white fields and, in the distance, caught sight of its glint on the sea.

When the car began to descend the steep, winding hill towards another little fishing village, she noticed passersby wave and Luke wave back with a cheery smile.

'You seem to know a lot of people,' Abigail commented.

'I've lived here all my life,' he said, braking as they rounded a bend. 'That's my school.'

She turned her head to see a small, granite building surrounded by a playground with a variety of climbing frames, slides and swings, that disappeared into a wide expanse of field.

'You went to school there?' she said. 'It doesn't look to have changed much over the years.'

He laughed.

'Oh, I can assure you, it has.'

'And now your own children go there, or are they too old?' she asked curiously.

Slowing the car to a halt and switching off the engine, he gave her a puzzled look.

'My own children? I don't have any, Abigail,' he said with a frown, and Abigail was more puzzled than ever.

She twisted in the leather seat to face him.

'But you mentioned the other morning at breakfast that you hadn't brought your children because they'd be too much for Great-Aunt Holly,' she said.

His shoulders shook with laughter and he

leaned forward to tilt her chin up to meet his eyes.

'Quite true,' he said, his eyes crinkling. 'There are a couple of hundred of them.'

He glanced across at the grey-stone building.

'I'm the headmaster here.'

Abigail felt heat burn into her face. How could she have been so stupid? It was so obvious, when you thought about it! She felt so embarrassed she didn't know what to say.

'So,' he said, undoing his car door, 'would you like to come and see where I live?'

Her feet slid on the slushy pavement as she stepped out, but Luke's arm caught her round the waist before she fell, and remained there while they climbed a narrow path.

From the outside, the house matched the grey granite of the neighbouring school, but once inside Abigail was surrounded by comfort. Deep, chintz-covered armchairs, none of which matched, worn rugs on polished, wooden floors, walls lined with books—all giving a warm sense of peace, something which she was aware of the minute she stepped inside.

'This, Abigail, is where I've always lived, ever since I was born. Nothing much has changed over the years as you can see, but it needs to do so,' Luke was saying, watching her reaction to his words intently.

He turned to rest his hands lightly on her

95

shoulders, and Abigail felt as though she had always known this house, and this man.

'Maybe one day, when you've had time to sort out your life, you and Flora will come back and help me change it into a family home again,' he said.

'One day,' she replied, raising her face to kiss him. 'One day, very soon, I promise.'

We hope you have enjoyed this Large Print book. Other Chivers Press or Thorndike Press Large Print books are available at your library or directly from the publishers.

For more information about current and forthcoming titles, please call or write, without obligation, to:

Chivers Large Print
published by BBC Audiobooks Ltd
St James House, The Square
Lower Bristol Road
Bath BA2 3BH
UK
email: bbcaudiobooks@bbc.co.uk
www.bbcaudiobooks.co.uk

OR

Thorndike Press
295 Kennedy Memorial Drive
Waterville
Maine 04901
USA
www.gale.com/thorndike
www.gale.com/wheeler

All our Large Print titles are designed for easy reading, and all our books are made to last.